Pearlie and her Pink Shell

WENDY HARMER

Illustrated by Gypsy Taylor

RANDOM HOUSE AUSTRALIA

For my truly magical mother.

Random House Australia Pty Ltd
Level 3, 100 Pacific Highway, North Sydney, NSW 2060
http://www.randomhouse.com.au

Sydney   New York   Toronto
London   Auckland   Johannesburg

First published by Random House Australia in 2008
Copyright © Out of Harms Way Pty Ltd 2008

National Library of Australia
Cataloguing-in-Publication Entry

Harmer, Wendy.
Pearlie and her pink shell.
ISBN 978 1 74166 143 9 (pbk).
I. Taylor, Gypsy. II. Title. (Series: Harmer, Wendy. Pearlie; 9)

A823.3

Designed and typeset by Jobi Murphy
Printed and bound by Everbest Printing Co. Ltd, China

It was a warm summer
afternoon in Jubilee Park.
The flowers were nodding and
the birds were resting in the shady trees.
Pearlie the park fairy had been up since dawn
making sure that everything was in its place,
just right. She was looking forward
to a refreshing cup of dew
and a lovely nap.

As she flew closer to her shell on the old stone fountain, Pearlie could see that there was one thing in Jubilee Park that was not right ... not right at all! The fountain was covered from top to bottom with giant steel poles and wooden ladders.

'Stars and moonbeams! What's happened here?' Pearlie wondered. She ducked through the tangle left by the Jubilee Park workmen and was alarmed to see her rosy pink shell had been freshly painted plain old grey!

'Oh no! Yuk!' exclaimed Pearlie. She didn't like the colour grey. It made her think of cold winter skies and wet dog hair. Pearlie couldn't imagine living in a house the colour of a rainy day. Straight away, she knew what she had to do.

'I'll just use my magic wand and change my shell back to perfect pink!' she said.

Being careful not to get her wings stuck in the wet paint, Pearlie popped inside her shell to find her wand.

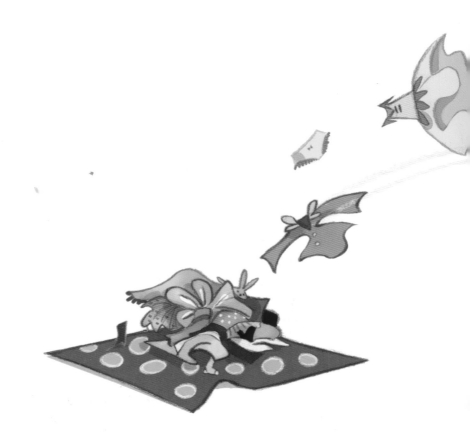

'Hurly, pheeeew, burly!' Pearlie wrinkled her tiny nose at the nasty wet-paint smell. She quickly looked about but couldn't find her wand anywhere. The awful fumes seemed to be getting worse. She bundled up some clothes and zoomed out the door.

'Cough, gasp!' Pearlie sat on a flower to catch her breath. There was simply no way she could go back inside her shell now. She would have to find somewhere to stay until the paint had dried.

Pearlie thought she might spend the night with
Jasper in his letterbox, so off she flew with her
bundle. From across the pond Pearlie could see a
huge cloud of dust swirling out of his front door.
In the middle of it was Jasper in dirty overalls.

'Hey, girlie Pearlie,' he sang. 'I'm doing some cool kitchen renovations.'

Pearlie peeped into Jasper's home and saw it was a jumble of sticks, sawdust and mud bricks.

'You can come for tea tomorrow when I've finished. Now, if you'll excuse me, I'd better get back to work.'

Jasper swung his magical elves' hammer. It was very loud indeed.

BANG!

'Good luck,' Pearlie shouted over the noise. 'Hmmm,' thought Pearlie. 'Perhaps I could go and stay with Great Aunt Garnet.'

Pearlie flew across the big city to Great Aunt Garnet's shop in the clock tower. There was a sign on the front door:

'Closed for the holidays.
xox Great Aunt Garnet.'

'Roots and twigs!' Pearlie puffed. By now her poor wings were starting to droop. There was one more place where she might find a bed. She headed back to Jubilee Park to Opal's tent in the desert garden.

When Pearlie arrived, she was most surprised to see Opal packing her suitcase.

'Gidday, Pearlie,' said Opal. 'Gee, you look like you could do with a rest!'

'Yes, I am really very tired,' replied Pearlie.

BANG! BANG!

'It's very noisy around here,' shouted Opal. 'I'm going home to Rainbow Ridge for the night until Jasper finishes hammering. Why don't you come with me?'

Pearlie thought this could be the answer to all her problems. She could stay with Opal, and when she came home she would get busy with her wand and change her home back to perfect pink. 'Thank you, Opal. I'd love to come,' she said.

After a delicious, cool Bunya nut shake, Pearlie and Opal set off on their long flight to the desert. They flew right over the city, through the bush, across the red sand and at last landed at Opal's home in Rainbow Ridge. That night Pearlie crawled into a soft bed of baby cockatoo feathers in Opal's cosy log. She looked out to the wide desert sky filled with stars shining like a million diamonds, and in a wink she was fast asleep.

The next day back at Jubilee Park, Jasper had finished his kitchen. He flew to Pearlie's shell to invite her to tea and was amazed to see that it was now painted an awful dull shade of grey.

'No way,' said Jasper. He saw the 'Wet Paint' sign and guessed that Pearlie must have gone away until it dried. Jasper knew Pearlie wouldn't like having a grey shell. Then he had a bright idea. 'I'll give Pearlie a very cool surprise,' he said.

He was back in his letterbox, looking in a cupboard for some pink paint, when Sapphire poked her head inside. 'I hope you've stopped that terrible banging!' she said rudely. 'I could hear it all the way to my place at the bottom of the garden. It gave me such a headache that I had to spend the whole day in bed!'

Jasper explained that he had finished his renovations and was now going to paint Pearlie's shell as a surprise.

Sapphire smiled to herself. She now had a plan of her own! 'Oh Jasper dear,' she said, 'why don't you have a nice rest? I'll take care of Pearlie's shell.'

Jasper wasn't sure this was such a good idea. Sapphire had been very naughty in the past.

'This is my chance to show Pearlie that I am a changed fairy by doing her a good deed,' said Sapphire sweetly. 'Please let me help.'

Jasper was very pleased to hear that Sapphire wanted to change her ways. He jumped into his spider-web hammock for a snooze. 'Sweet,' he said as he closed his eyes.

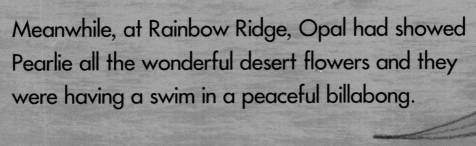

Meanwhile, at Rainbow Ridge, Opal had showed
Pearlie all the wonderful desert flowers and they
were having a swim in a peaceful billabong.

'Twirly-whirly, the desert is a truly beautiful
place,' sighed Pearlie as she stretched out
on a rock in the sun.

But what Pearlie did not know was, at that very moment, those two flea-infested felons, Scrag and Mr Flea, were climbing up the poles and ladders on the old stone fountain.

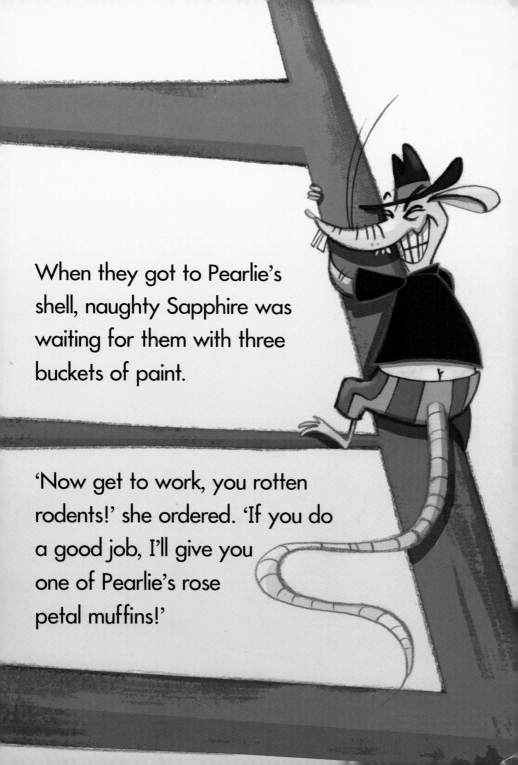

When they got to Pearlie's shell, naughty Sapphire was waiting for them with three buckets of paint.

'Now get to work, you rotten rodents!' she ordered. 'If you do a good job, I'll give you one of Pearlie's rose petal muffins!'

'Oooh, muffins!' said Mr Flea greedily. 'Can I have seven?'

'Yeah,' cackled Scrag, 'and after our feast we'll relax in Pearlie's bath.'

'With lots of stinky bubbles!' Mr Flea clapped his filthy yellow claws.

Sapphire laughed wickedly. 'When you've finished, she'll never want to live here again. Then I can move in and declare myself Queen of Jubilee Park!'

Sapphire zapped the rats' bottoms with her wand.

'Yikes!' they squealed and immediately got to work.

It was the middle of the afternoon at Rainbow Ridge when Pearlie decided it was time to go home. 'Your home is truly beautiful, Opal, but my shell should be dry by now,' she said.

'No worries. Let's go,' replied Opal. They packed their things and made the journey back to Jubilee Park.

As she came closer and closer to the old stone fountain, Pearlie was shocked to see her shell. It was now painted in horrible purple and green stripes with bright orange spots! 'Eeek!' cried Pearlie.

'Crikey!' exclaimed Opal.

At that moment Scrag and Mr Flea stuck their horrid furry heads out her front door. 'Hey! How do you like our paint job, Miss Pearlie Pants?' called Scrag.

'Yeah, it's sooo pretty!' laughed Mr Flea. 'Pretty disgusting, that is!'

Now Pearlie rubbed her wings together and her green eyes flashed. 'You take off my clothes and come out of my shell this instant!' she demanded.

'Go away! We're living here now! And you can't zap us with your silly wand this time, Pearlie,' Mr Flea yelled.

'That's right! Because we found it under your bed.' Scrag waved Pearlie's wand. 'And we're never giving it back. Ha, ha, ha!' He chewed on the handle just to make Pearlie extra mad.

'Grrrr!' Pearlie was mad all right – madder than she'd ever been in her whole life! But what could she do without her wand?

Pearlie and Opal thought it was best to go to Jasper's house and ask him to help. Between the three of them they would surely be able to kick those rats out of Pearlie's shell!

Sapphire saw Pearlie and Opal race past her. She sneaked off to the fountain and hid in the long grass to watch the fun.

Later, inside Pearlie's shell, Mr Flea was sitting in the bath and burping loudly. An empty muffin tin was on the floor. Scrag was relaxing on Pearlie's bed and chewing his revolting toenails.

BANG! BANG! BANG!

Scrag got such a fright he fell on the floor.
'What was that? Get out of the bath and have
a look,' he growled at Mr Flea.

Up on top of Pearlie's shell, Jasper was banging
loudly with his elves' hammer.

As soon as Mr Flea popped his head out, Opal
swung her magic rope, Pearlie tied it around and
around his fat gut, and they had him captured!
Opal quickly lowered Mr Flea to the ground
with her rope and then pulled it undone. Mr Flea
untangled himself and ran off as fast as he could.
One rat gone and one to go!

BANG! BANG! BANG!

'Aaaargh!' Scrag covered his scruffy ears with his sharp claws. 'Stop that rotten racket!' He grabbed the tins of paint, rushed out the door and threw them. He aimed at Pearlie ... and missed. Down, down went the buckets of paint into the long grass.

Jasper spied his scabby snout. 'There he is,' he shouted. 'Get him!'

Quick as a flash, Pearlie was on top of Scrag. Once again Opal threw her rope. She missed! Scrag scrambled up onto the roof of Pearlie's shell and Jasper tried to grab him. Scrag ducked, then he tripped over his tail and tumbled head-first into the water way below.

Scrag screeched! He swam to the edge as fast as he could, jumped out and tore off through the park. Two rats gone!

'HOORAY!!' Pearlie, Opal and Jasper cheered.

Just then, Jasper saw Sapphire in the grass covered in purple, green and orange paint. 'So this was your surprise for Pearlie? Serves you right, man!' he laughed.

Sapphire scowled and stomped off with soggy wings to her home at the bottom of the garden.

Jasper and Opal worked all afternoon
to help their friend Pearlie tidy her shell.
'And now,' announced Pearlie, 'for the best bit!'
She waved her precious wand and,
in an instant, Pearlie's shell glowed
a beautiful rosy shade of pink
in the moonlight.

Later that evening the three friends sat down
to supper.

'There's no place like home,' giggled Pearlie as
she raised a glass of daisy fizz. 'Especially when
it's perfectly pink!'